CITY
LIMITS

FRAMED

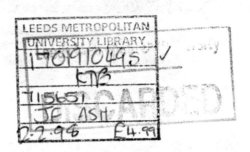
ORCHARD BOOKS
96 Leonard Street, London EC2A 4RH
Orchard Books Australia
14 Mars Road, Lane Cove, NSW 2066
ISBN 1 86039 406 X (hardback)
ISBN 1 86039 576 7 (paperback)
First published in Great Britain 1997
First paperback publication 1998
Text © Bernard Ashley 1997
The right of Bernard Ashley to be identified as the author of
this work has been asserted by them in accordance with the
Copyright, Designs and Patents Act, 1988.
A CIP catalogue record for this book is available from the
British Library.
Printed in Great Britain

Bernard Ashley

CITY LIMITS

FRAMED

ORCHARD BOOKS

Chapter One

When it came to being tactful Mack had a touch as light as a fist in the face. Where other people gave a wink, he mugged his head off; when a whisper was favourite, he gave out with station announcements; when shaking hands was the drill, he jumped on your back. He just hadn't got the knack of keeping things *dinky*.

This afternoon in Renny's City Limits Café, his old mate Dean wanted to crown him with a black sack – pulled well down. They all knew they'd got a famous face sitting over there – Dean and Sharon and Kwai had clocked him straight off, coming in – and they'd winked and elbowed each other on the quiet, so the guy wouldn't feel stared at. But when the penny dropped for Mack, didn't he have to bounce his news off the wall? Do dogs bark?

"'E's off the telly!" he told the place, pulling a face like a monkey eating nougat, just as if he were keeping the news discreet. As if!

Of course the Face heard him – the whole city could have heard him – but with no more than a creak of his leather top the man continued fizzing along with a string of tried and trusted chat show stories to entertain the people at his table.

"Hoo–hoo–hoo!" Dean blew quietly down the neck of a Coke.

Even Sharon found it hard to keep a head of steam while he was doing his act. Which made it less likely than ice in the Sahara that she was going to be impressed by the man.

"That hot dog don't need no mustard!" she snorted into her bottle.

"What've I seen 'im in?" Mack asked the area north of the Thames.

But Renny was coming round from behind the café counter, wiggling his fingers at them.

"Sssh!" He picked up a doughnut and posted it into Mack's mouth. "They're my customers!"

Renny was Dean's dad, the Italian owner of the City Limits Café. He liked having Dean's friends in early evenings, when he wasn't so busy: he liked to let them have their table and their laughs; kept them topped up with burps. It was "family", Italian style, the way he'd spent his own young days.

Here, the kids would stay an hour or so before going off to follow their fancies. But they had to remember that City Limits was a business — and if you made the customers edgy, they might just edge themselves on out of the door. Waiting for trains or taking five from their city office, people didn't want too much "jangle".

Renny gave a last warning waggle, and went back to his *espresso* machine. It was five o'clock — quiet time — and this was the second afternoon City Limits had been graced by the Face. Renny wanted the two night gig to turn into a run.

But Mack suddenly went off bang again: exploding sugar all over the table. "Adam something!" he cried. "Got 'im! Adam Bond!"

Adam Bond, the Face, turned round as he got up and bowed at his name. "Back to it, slaves!" he told the theatricals. And he led the way out, straight off up the pavement, not holding the door for any of the rest.

"They're at *Pepys Above*." Kwai had been quiet, which was her style. But it wasn't the style of the others, who, counting Mack out of it, had been paralysed today by the star performance. "All this month."

"Then we hope they come back. If we can send Mack to Scotland, or somewhere!" Renny liked to pretend he thought Mack was from the real north, instead of just north of the river.

Pepys Above was a studio theatre, over the Samuel Pepys pub down the road – rubbish one week and rave reviews in the posh papers the next. And sometimes the actors would use City Limits as a Green Room instead of the Samuel Pepys bar, just to change the scene.

"Can't wait to miss *that* show!" Sharon said.

"Yeah, why are they always so *loud*?" Mack

wanted to know, top of his voice. "Actors?"

"Actors *and* the rest!" Renny waggled another warning finger at him. "I don't hear all that. They're business — I just hear my till ringing."

Chapter Two

Business or not, the crew were less keen still the next day. Bighead celebs were one thing, but ducky little stuck-up actresses their own age were something else.

This one had the look of a vase you could crack just by staring at it; a skin you could see through, it had to have one layer less than everyone else. Her eyes were the sort of blue you could have painted-in with a couple of drops left over from the Willow Pattern. And there wasn't a mark on her face, no zit, no mole, no freckle, no blot of any sort. Look at her and then look at Mack and it was like panning from an ice rink to a demolition site. Up against her *everyone* looked rough, and the black Sharon and Chinese Kwai were beauties enough; and Dean himself could thump a heart when he gave anyone the eye. Of her type, the girl was perfect. And doesn't the world just adore perfect things?

"Stop me giving that puss a slap!" Sharon told Dean, gripping his arm – in case he was looking over at the girl with any notions of his own. "She been *erased*, or what?"

Dean looked over at the table of luvvies, sitting where they'd sat before, Adam Bond, the Face, still singing his territory over there like a bossy blackbird. Holding forth, but with more bizz than buzz today, yattering on about the play.

The girl had her back to them, facing into a mirror on the café wall. She'd asked for ice and lemon, and was pouring fizzy water into a glass. A *glass*?

"Lady Muck!" Sharon said, snorting up the dregs from the bottom of her bottle. "Ain't she got no suck?"

Dean nodded that he'd noticed the girl, then looked away, fast. When Sharon gave you a poke in the ribs you went direct to Intensive Care on life support. But never mind her beauty, that quick look had told him the girl was one of our miserable sisters. She was giving all her attention to her glass as if drinking the water were the cherry of life. She listened to the Face without nodding, and she spoke without looking up.

"Yes."

She was next to a dumpy young-but-old woman who was forever fiddling in her bag;

and on her other side was a broom handle of a man with hair which had to be a hang-up-at-night job. He was making notes in an organiser – maroon, wouldn't you know?

"Hi, everyone!"

The girl looked up, with the rest. Angelica had come down from upstairs, out of school uniform, homework done, and bouncing her pretty little curls to prove it.

Renny made sure his little angel had a pulp of fresh orange to suck into.

"Is he the big man?" Angelica whispered – ten years old sounding twenty. "Leather jacket?"

Renny's hand went over Mack's mouth like a cap on an oil blow.

Everyone nodded, louder than talking, and getting another turn of the head from Miss Perfect.

"'Cos Mum's made him up," Angelica

hoarsed on. "London Weekend Television."

Dean's and Angelica's mother did part-time make-up at the South Bank studios.

"She says he's longer in the chair than Joan Collins."

"Ssssh!" Renny risked taking his hand off Mack's mouth. "That's a show biz secret, like the confession."

He went, with another of his finger wags, and the place busied up a bit. Renny took a couple of orders and got his knife to salami slicing. A "him and her" couple of city whizzers came into the café and were straight into their attaché cases for files – the man just about old enough to shave, and her looking at him like she wouldn't mind finding out for sure sometime. Then she saw the Face and did a mime behind her portfolio; which young shaver couldn't respond to because of the distraction of another customer coming in.

But this one wasn't a paying customer. She was from Pepys Upstairs, come to call the actors back.

"Arif's ready for you to see the set," she told the Face. "And you're wanted to read Act One before we call it a day..."

She had a slight limp – and the sure foot-edness of a stage manager. They *would* read Act One, and the Face *would* check the set.

Now the young city shaver recognised the celeb and died on a shred of salami.

"Have you met Lucy?" the Face asked the stage manager. He was giving Miss Perfect a sweeping intro like Des O'Connor. But the girl hardly looked up.

The stage manager let go of the door and offered a hand to Miss Perfect, while Wig-on-a-Broomstick paid the bill, out of his purse.

"Brenda Tate," the stage manager said to the girl. "SM" – letting the rank show.

"Lucy Mesurier-Gull," the girl came back, trumping company rank with her hyphen. "The daughter in the play."

"Oh, I know the play." Brenda Tate had reversed and was back out of the door, quickly followed by the rest; the Face out last wearing his *famous* look for the punters.

The young shaver was still dying, and Angelica had just seen her juice grabbed as Sharon downed it to stop her own choke.

"You hear that? *Mesurier-Gull*!" Sharon wheezed through the tears in her eyes. "Give me *air*! More like Misery Guts!"

Chapter Three

Misery Guts was in without the Face next afternoon. Perhaps he'd had a bad day and settled for a stiff one in the Samuel Pepys. But, whatever, the girl was sitting on her own with her young-but-old chaperone – and weren't things quiet? Renny's little Sanyo could actually be heard.

Mack's Auntie Pearl was dishing up an East End meal that night – cockles and whelks from the Lanes, followed by eel pie and mash;

a little thank you to the kids for a favour they'd done her. So it was only a quick meet-up, kneeling and leaning, instead of sitting; hanging on for Sharon who always went by Greenwich *Generous* Time.

With no Face and no Sharon, and Mack worried about Auntie Pearl's menu, "Quiet" had a capital Q. And there wasn't much chat, either, between the girl and her minder; no way were those two fluttering together like birds of a feather. The girl was stuck into a script, every now and then her lips going at it rosary-like, and her minder was forever into her hold-all like a horse at a feed bag.

Renny served an All-Day Breakfast to his regular chuckie-egg-down-his-tie man and stopped by their table on the way back.

"Oh, er, a black tea for me, and, er –" The woman found a scrap of paper curled at the bottom of her bag, hardly bothered looking up, waved a hand at the girl for her to order what she wanted.

"Water, please. Still. *A ghiaccio*." Renny did a little bow to salute the Italian. Not that he'd make much of a living if people only ever wanted tap water with ice.

Dean heard the lingo. "Clock Misery Guts showing off!" he told Mack – who *had* to look round, didn't he, as if she might be doing cartwheels.

But Mack was really taken up with the time on the KitKat clock. Auntie Pearl would be starting on the whelks solo if they didn't get off quick.

Angelica was the only one sitting. She hadn't been in on the Auntie Pearl thing, wasn't invited. She was stuffing a consolation slice of cream gâteau down her throat, plastering it round her mouth on its way inside.

Sharon suddenly bowled in through the door.

"Get me to that feast, brethren!"

For a million pounds she couldn't enter anywhere quietly. One day her wedding would be the indoor version of the Notting Hill Carnival. *Here, RAH, comes the bride, RAH RAH!*

Right now she looked wicked in a fluorescent off-the-shoulder top and short black skirt. She posed in the doorway like the Statue of Liberty, waiting for the flash bulbs to crackle.

Mack looked down at his crumpled T-shirt and old jeans. "I'll eat out on the landing," he offered.

But Kwai was pulling him to the door; she wasn't dressed up so special herself; and Dean had that sipping-boiling-water face on that said his girlfriend might just have gone over the top. By a couple of air miles.

"*Ciao*, Renny!" Sharon called over the

counter. "Wish me luck with them ol' cockles!"

"I wish you a quiet life," Renny replied. "And the same for me, too."

And they were gone. The All-Day-Breakfast had already egged-up his tie in the buzz so he was going cross-eyed down his nose wiping up with his *San Pellegrino*.

Lucy Mesurier-Gull hadn't seemed to lift her eyes from her script, but if anyone were noticing, she was still on the page she'd first opened. And now Minder had fished out her mobile.

"Luce, I'm just going to make a call." Which wouldn't need saying, her with the thing in her hand, if it weren't that this call was going to be made in the doorway outside. Something closet. "It's a bit noisy in here." Well, it had been, but it wasn't any more. She went outside and started tapping her Motorola.

Renny carried her black tea in its Russian glass to her place; but before he could turn back to get the girl's water, Angelica was up and taking it for him.

"*Grazie.*"

"*Prego.*" Angelica put the glass in front of the girl. And instead of backing off with the reward of a sudden sunshine smile, she sat up in Minder's seat.

"He's my dad."

"I guessed."

"Angelica Sophia Romita."

The girl shut her script, looked hard and serious at Angelica. "Lucy Misery Guts." And she held out her hand for a shake.

Chapter Four

Angelica had the face of someone who didn't know whether to bust a gut or wet herself.

She busted a gut. She snorted with false laughter. She cackled in her throat and had to grab a gulp of Lucy's water.

Chukkie, the All-Day-Breakfast, lost another drip of egg, down his flies.

"Misery Guts? That is what they call me, isn't it?"

"No!" A couple of beats. "Yeah. But only

for fun. It's all only for fun with them." But Angelica's face had *in the hot seat* written all over it.

"They look fun."

"How do you know? You never look at us."

"Mirrors." Lucy explained to a blank face. "When you go to stage school you spend all day in front of these big mirrors. They teach you dancing with their backs to you, looking past themselves in the glass. You live a mirror sort of life." Lucy looked as if she'd suddenly hit on some great truth.

Out of the door, her minder was puffed up like a red balloon, smiling and batting her eyes as if whoever was on the other end could see her. She looked as if right now she didn't know whether it was Thursday, Friday or Rosh Hashanah. A bus could have run up the pavement past her and she wouldn't have seen it.

"What you doing? You full-time at the theatre?" Angelica wanted to know.

Lucy nodded. "Drama school, really – but I've got this part in the play. I'm the daughter."

"Bet it's good doing that. With that man. My mum's made him up; London Weekend Television."

"It's all right."

"*All right?* I'd be dancing round the walls!"

Lucy looked out of the door. Things were still popping like champagne out there on the mobile. She put her hands flat on the table, signals of truth, and swore Angelica to secrecy with a clear blue look.

The girl crossed her heart and wished to die.

"He's a bully," Lucy said. "Mr Adam Bond. All this luvvie stuff in here is a show."

"He don't hit you, does he?"

"No, let him try! But he shouts. And he

swears. And he treats you like something stuck under his shoe."

Angelica worked it out, a bit too loud. "Oh, dog's muck," she said.

Which had Renny looking up and Chuckie getting out while he still had a suit to wear home.

Lucy showed half a centimetre of space between a finger and a thumb. "He made me look *this* big yesterday, and my nerve's gone. It's like I can't do anything right. A bit more of this and I'll get replaced."

Angelica, the little mother, patted Lucy's hand. "Go on!" she said. "You'll be all right. What is it they say? 'Break an arm'?"

"A leg. 'Break a leg'."

"Yeah, well, that too. Break both. An' while you're at it, break his neck!" Which gave her the giggles and she had to dive back into Lucy's water.

Lucy's own snort of laughter wasn't very stage school.

"Right, Luce, come on!" Minder had lit a cigarette and was standing inside the doorway, her neck all blotchy. "Act Two."

Which was Lucy's call. And she went, the smile wiped off her face, looking like a lamb going to the slaughter.

The way to Auntie Pearl's went past the Samuel Pepys. And while Mack got all *agitato* that the first course would have been eaten off the menu by the time they got to the flat, Dean just had to stop and take a look at the posters for the play.

They were all the same, and all Adam Bond. The Face stared moodily out with just a rhubarb of wording squeezed down the side.

"Yeah, that's 'im. Come on!" Mack went off up the pavement but had to come back.

"It's him but it's not him, really," said Kwai, her head on the tilt.

"Him in his dreams! Years back!" Sharon pointed a jangly arm at the poster. "Be like me sticking a baby picture on my bus pass an' saying it's me."

"Be good!" said Dean. "On a rug, bare bum?"

For which he got pushed so hard he went through the door of the downstairs bar and almost had to buy a round of drinks.

The Face was at a table with Brenda, the SM – two pairs of spectacles poring over a marked-up script.

"Some neighbourhood for a theatre!" the actor said, as Dean scrambled himself out. "And where's that ruddy girl?"

Only Mack being in a hurry prevented a

pavement wrestling match between Dean and Sharon – Mack being in a hurry *and* the distant sight of Misery Guts and her Minder scurrying towards the Samuel Pepys.

"Come *on*!" he commanded. "She's gone to a lot of bother, Auntie Pearl. You in for this or not?"

And because they were, they left the scene, quick.

"'Take five', I said, not fifteen!" was what Lucy got from Adam – as if it had been her and not Minder who had held him up. Which didn't help.

Minder hurried Lucy in and up the narrow stairs to the theatre.

Except *theatre* was a bit West End for this place; it was only what used to be called a Function Room – something on a very long elastic from the Theatre Royal, Drury Lane.

At one end there were ten lines of tip-up

cinema seats on a little slope, facing the stage
– with its drawing room set and its ceiling
hung with dust and Strand lights.

The rest of the cast were sitting in the tip-
ups smoking, knitting, reading, bored as oil-
holes.

"Lucy, *sweet!*" said her stage mother as Lucy
came in, but she didn't look up from her *Word
Puzzler*. Amanda Flowers. More like Amanda
Weed, the way she smoked.

"Right, loves, now we're *all* here..."

And the tart way Adam Bond looked at
her, the big telly fish in this small pond, he
who could not put a foot wrong, made Lucy's
stomach churn – and she knew she was going
to act the way a ballerina dances when she's
wearing wellingtons. Nothing turning out the
way it should. And her confidence was like a
colander, with more holes in it than there had
ever been steel holding it together.

Chapter Five

Auntie Pearl had laid on a good tuck-in. And, as Mack had feared, she'd also laid into it, waiting. In a sparky continental mood, a mix of Left-bank Paris and the Mile End Road, she'd enjoyed a fair share of the whelks with a few glasses of something white and sparkling – and we're not talking lemonade.

Not that she was ever the worse for a drop of shampoo. It just seemed to have the effect of opening an extra button on her blouse.

"*Entrez! Entrez!*" she said in her high French. And, while Mack saw to the Cokes in an impersonation of Renny, she got them going on the seafood. Which wasn't easy to eat for novices, but which Kwai got the hang of fast while Sharon made a good pretence – and Dean went home with more stuffed in his trouser pocket than lining his stomach. A special skill.

"We got 'eld up at the Pepys," Mack told Auntie Pearl as she re-heated the eel pie.

"More than I will for the foreseeable!" she came back.

"Why's that?" It was her local: she had her own corner in there. Mick the barman would get an invite to her funeral.

"Why? You seen? They've opened up the upstairs again; the bar's stuffed with *theatricals*." She said it as if the word stood for something you had to disinfect. "Not the old place at all at present."

She cut and dolloped, onto their plates. "And as for Mr High-an'-Mighty..."

"'E's the one I told you about. Off the telly..."

"Oh, and doesn't he think he's the last word!" Auntie Pearl could do a good lah-di-dah face. "The big 'I am'!"

"Why, what's 'e done to you?"

They were back at the table now, Dean, Sharon and Kwai looking at the eel pie as if it might wriggle to life, jump up and electrocute them.

"Clicks his fingers, shouts his orders. 'Michael, Michael' he *will* call Mick. Thinking being famous will save him the price of a round!"

"Well, 'e *is* on the box."

"That's not famous." She slid everyone a plate of steaming pie and mash, smiled at each like a TV chef. "Lovely! What a taste, you'll enjoy that."

Which they tried to; while Auntie Pearl, who'd over-done it on the first course, sat with a fag, waving away the smoke in a genteel way and going on about Adam Bond, the Face.

"I'm not as young as I look," she said. "I know him from old, before he changed his name. I saw him once in a kids' show he'd pay me to forget..."

And to cover what they weren't quite managing to get down of the eel pie, Dean and Sharon started pressing her on what that was – anything to take her attention off their non-eating.

But they didn't need to bother. Having given her all to the cooking and the first course, Auntie Pearl asked to get down from the table and sat herself in her armchair;

whose soft comfort soon had her open-mouthed and breathing deeply.

Mack wanted to wake her up, out of politeness to her guests, but the others wouldn't hear of it. At least, not until they'd washed up and put the kitchen bunny-sack of left-overs down the chute.

By the next afternoon, Angelica had had it with all the "Auntie Pearl and seafood" talk. She hadn't been with them – and what could be more gutty than trying to share in something you hadn't shared in?

It was a let-off when Misery Guts and her minder came in. Angelica waggled her fingers across at Lucy like a bride showing the ring, but Lucy didn't seem to see. Her face had got some colour for a change – it was red around the eyes, and puffy. Never mind a glass of still water with ice, she looked as if what she wanted was a river to jump in. She sat herself with her back to the café.

Two minutes, and her minder was out in the doorway again, bashing her mobile. And even Angelica knew why Lucy was here. She was being dragged about by that woman like a dog on a lead – taken for a walk as an excuse for Minder to rabbit to her secret boyfriend.

By now, Dean could see that Mack was going with the laugh only up to a point; after all, it *was* his Auntie Pearl's supper that they were hammering.

"Anyway, old Kwai looked a treat, going at her whelks like a born Eastender," he said, daring a smile at her. But Sharon saw it and got him under the table.

"Ow!"

And Angelica went. She skidded her chair

back and flashed over to Lucy.

"Come on, Luce," she said. No messing about, straight in. Come and say hello to our lot." Putting a sock in the seafood talk would be Angelica's gift to City Limits.

Lucy didn't want to budge; but actors aren't up to much if they can't take themselves across a room to meet new people. So she picked up her water, and went.

"Alert! Misery Guts!" Seeing her coming, Sharon looked like someone with a fly flown into her mouth. Kwai caught a dose of the instant hiccups. Dean snapped a bar of KitKat loud enough to start the hundred metres.

"This is Lucy." Angelica sweetly rearranged everyone's chairs with pokes in tender places. They rearranged their own faces.

"Hi!" said Lucy, throwing herself in bravely.

The mumble back could have been in

low Latin.

"Angelica thinks I need to make some friends."

"An' what's *your* thinking on that, sistuh?" Sharon asked her.

"The same as hers – especially when the friends you've already got *care* so much!" She flicked her head at Minder, who was dribbling into her mobile outside. "If she goes on much longer she'll dissolve that thing."

"Given the woman don't eat it first," said Sharon.

"Yeah – sort of, *rabbit* pie," said Kwai.

"Doner ke*blab*," said Dean.

"Chicken *chat*," said Mack.

And a short silence.

"I suppose it depends what number she *daal*ed," said Lucy.

And the crack of laughing had Renny up from a bend at the deli.

Now Lucy had to have a Coke, which Dean fetched, because City Limits kids didn't drink *water* – lemon, iced, fizzy or spa. Angelica snuggled in next to her like a teddy in bed – well, Lucy was *her* friend first.

"What you doin' with ol' Face-ache, then?" Sharon wanted the word. "Don' look like it's 'Jumpin' Harlem' you're performing round there."

"With my skin?" Lucy *was* transparent pale. "They'd think they were looking at negatives."

Sharon laughed and they slapped hands. "Right on!"

And it seemed that Lucy was in. Except, coming through the door was the Face himself. In role as the heavy. He caught Minder by the arm as he came and swung her in like a hostage, snapping shut her mobile on a choked "goodbye".

"We're waiting for this girl again!" he

told her.

"I'm sorry, Adam," the woman started on. "She was just getting on nicely with some friends..."

"Friends are not on her licence and not in the contract!"

But Lucy was already on her feet, chasséing the tables to get to where she'd left her script.

"*And*, little lady –"

She froze in his cold spotlight.

"*Study!* In the profession, when we're less than perfect, luv, we use short breaks to brush up on our lines. We *work*, so we don't let the company down. Because nothing *comes. Off* the stage we strive to be good *on* the stage. And you're far from that, dear. *Far* from it."

A strong speech. It could have brought down the curtain on an act. And the most humiliating public thing Dean and the rest had ever heard outside a classroom. Their faces looked like they were eating eel pie again.

Adam Bond held open the door for Minder to scuttle under his arm; and for Lucy to follow, who was outright crying now. Never mind holding anything back – long before she got to the street she was all nose and teardrops.

Face-ache waved at Renny. "I'm so sorry."

"*Please*, someone make sure you are!" Sharon snapped.

"The dog!" from Dean.

"The rat!" from Kwai.

"I'd just like 'im to meet my dad!" from Mack.

"But your dad's dead," they all told him, one voice.

"'S'actly what I mean."

But from now on Auntie Pearl's eel pie was right off the conversation menu. In its place was a tastier dish – called *hating Adam Bond*.

Chapter Six

Angelica was in on things now. That night, when her mother crept in after doing make-up for the late-night weather girl, her little angel was as wide awake as Christmas Eve. Sitting up like a new doll.

"That pig!" she said.

Sophia Romita took a deep breath. Dean? Renny? Who was Pig of the Day today? But this time the girl wasn't having a moan about one of the wicked men indoors. This pig was outside the sty.

"Adam Bond. He treated Lucy like she was dog's muck under his shoe. In front of everyone!"

Sophia sat on the bed.

"Stinking! He's always jumping down her throat. He won't give her a chance to get good."

"*Mama-mia!*" Sophia said. "She won't be the first to go to pieces when she's needled with nerves. My weather girl talked about 'rind and wain' tonight; which threw her, 'blowing away any early morning frog'."

"He was a bully!" Angelica persisted; she wasn't going to be put off by some studio joke. "He made my mouth go all salty; made me want to hit him."

"You didn't, did you?"

"No!"

Sophia said a quick little *grazie* to the ceiling.

"'Cos we've got a better idea."

"We? Who?" Perhaps Sophia's *grazie* had come a bit too soon.

"Me and Dean and Mack and Sharon and Kwai."

"Oh?" Sophia sat on the edge of her bed. "Are you in the gang now?" Kids grew up so quickly these days; this was her little angel, only yesterday a baby in her arms. She stroked the long locks now spread on the pillow.

"Not really, I'm sort of... on the edge. But you can help."

"*Me?* To get you in the gang or to help this Lucy?"

"Both. But mainly helping Lucy; that's what I really want."

"Well, then, I suppose you're going to tell me how..." And, tired as she was, Sophia sat and heard the girl out. Weren't mothers meant to be best friends with their daughters?

City East had its own community newspaper. It came through the door every Wednesday, free – adverts and local this-and-that; what was on at the flicks, gigs and venues, where to eat, that sort of thing. A year or so before, they'd done a feature on Renny's City Limits Café, which Renny had kept in a picture frame till it went as yellow as an old leaf – the deal for which was that Renny took a small advert in the paper every week. It was nothing big and pricey, but a little reminder for the businesses in their part of the city that he did take-away hot and cold snacks, baguettes and deli for all their busy-busy execs.

Now Dean and Sharon dug out the editor in her office over a car showroom. They chose the lunch hour on press day – when the paper was on the streets and she wouldn't be so busy – and they wore their school uniforms to give themselves the cred they reckoned they wanted.

They had two weapons besides; Renny's regular ad, which he was thinking of taking for a second year, and the fact that papers always like to grab the youth; young people today being the readers and advertisers of tomorrow.

Plus, Dean and Sharon were part of the ethnic mix. They couldn't fail.

"There's a play at the Pepys Upstairs," Deanopened with. *Save Tomorrow For Me.*

"Not an exam text, is it?" The editor, a washed out young woman who looked as if she were the entire staff, started grabbing at a basket of press releases.

"Don't think so —"

"But there's a teen edge to it? Isn't there a girl...?" She wasn't going to give up her riffling.

Till Sharon chimed in. "Leave that. I'll tell

you what it is."

The editor left it.

"There's this dude face in the play. Adam Bond?"

"Ye…es…" The editor had been in the wrong basket. Now she flipped out a glossy of the actor from a picture pile.

"Oooh!" Sharon put on a mock faint. "Ye…e…s! That's the guy. He's a real big name with the kids; I tell you, our school's goin' *poppin'* over him!"

"Really?" The editor turned the glossy sideways to see what the attraction could be.

"*Phe–nomenon!*"

She had the glossy upside down now.

"No tellin' ever, is there? Like *Jerusalem* hitting the charts, Christmas."

"You're right. There's never any telling." But the editor's eyes were asking, "*So?*"

"So we hope we're the first, asking to meet

him, do an interview."

"For your school magazine? But that's not for me to say…"

"No, for you. For *City Echo*. For the *Youf*."

"Ah!"

"Sort of, Job Experience," Dean cut in. "My dad, you know, City Limits, regular advert on page eight, he said we should ask you first." Hinting that it might be the *Sun* or the *Mirror* if not; plus a cancelled ad.

"Well – why not?" The editor was making notes on a *While You Were Out*. "You got shorthand?" she asked Sharon.

"No, regular length…" That girl couldn't resist some things; questions like that were like jelly babies to a toddler.

Dean's smile hurt him.

"…But we got a tape machine. There won't be no probs."

"Fine. Well, we can set it up, I'm sure. Might

even sell it on to one of the kiddie mags. And I should think he'll be keen as mustard. Adam Bond."

"Oh, he'll be cooking!" Sharon said. "Cook-*king*!"

"I'll take your word for it – but I've got to say I don't see the pull myself." She was even looking on the back of the picture now, in case there was some clue there.

"But then, you ain't quite the *youf*, are you?"

On which note Dean led Sharon out, before she blew it.

Chapter Seven

It was Saturday morning, and the play was getting to the crucial stage, where no one carried a script any more and all the little bits of "business" were being given the Mr Sheen. It should have been the best part of the rehearsals; but Lucy was still asking her soul whether she should ever have gone in for acting at all.

She'd felt like Broadway when she'd got the part, after being recommended by Mrs Moon at the Garrick Academy. And she still turned some of the other kids' faces green, coming out to the Pepys every day instead of going to classes. It could have been a dream.

But now she hated it. Adam Bond, the old tart, had decided to make the dream a nightmare. To balloon his own ego he'd pricked her confidence, which got worse each time she stepped on to the stage.

How long could it be before she was sent back to Garrick in disgrace, for the mobile Lover to do the return journey with a replacement – someone like Gretchen Thomas, who'd turn Smug into a whole new body language?

It was only the old Mesurier-Gull guts that had Lucy wanting to dig in and fight against that.

"Right, everyone!" A clap of Brenda the SM's hands. "We're going to run Act One."

"Overture and beginners!" coughed Amanda Flowers, over Lucy. "Don't be late on your entrance, sweet, else we're left standing there counting the empty seats."

"OK."

"Listen hard, and start to move when I'm halfway through your cue. Pace, pace, pace!"

Lucy nodded, and took her place behind the scenery flat with the door in it, staring at the balsa and wondering why the heck anyone should ever want to do this for a living.

Downstairs, Kwai was coming through the bar. She followed the arrow on the "THEATRE" sign and went for the stairs, up and round, to put her nose through the dusty curtain into the theatre.

What she saw was a brightly lit stage

dressed up as a country house drawing room. There was no sign of Lucy – but tons of Adam Bond who was standing in the middle of the stage having a row with one of the women who'd been in City Limits with him. Except, this row had to be pretend – because these two were actually letting each other get a word in, which wasn't at all the way Kwai's mum and dad went on.

All the same, Kwai could feel a real edge in the place. If she'd stuck her hands out flat they would have trembled, like trying to make two opposite ends of a magnet meet.

She crept further in, stood still. And the stage arguing suddenly stopped. The man and the woman had frozen, staring into each other's faces, as there came a sudden thumping and a pushing on the scenery door.

"Well, come in, then!" Adam Bond exploded. "We're standing here like a couple of spares!"

"It won't open!"

It was Lucy's voice from behind the door; with another bang and shake which looked like it could bring the scenery down all together.

"It's stuck."

"It is not stuck! We've re-hung it, *remember*?!" The Face was over there and at it like Old Bill on a dawn raid. "It opens *out*! When are you going to start paying attention?"

"I wasn't here when you did that…"

"No, round at the café, no doubt! You silly little cow!" Adam Bond spun back in a rage; King Lear, Othello and Tom Cat with a singed tail, all rolled into one.

Which was when he saw Kwai standing there.

"You! If you've come for the take-away order, you can take *this* one away for a start!"

He was waving an arm at Lucy. But the

hurt wasn't only in her; it went as deep as bone marrow into Kwai. Why should her Chinese face only trigger "take-away" in this ignorant bully's mind? He was the sort who'd give living under a stone a bad name. If Kwai had had butterflies about coming here for the gang, they flew away now. Let this creep do the worrying!

But she kept her voice polite. "I've come about the interview. The editor said to check with a Mr Bond." Give him that for a start, "*a* Mr Bond" – not "*the*".

"Yes?" He came down, a big starry sigh. "Now that we've stopped…"

"The interview for the *City Echo*; it's to fix up when."

"Ah." Adam Bond turned to the rest of the company, who were lolling. "Publicity. Every little helps." But the look on his face was eager for Number One. "The editor thinks she can sell it on to *Time Out*."

"Is tomorrow OK? About three?"

"Sure, yes, fine, it's OK with me. Get sharpening your pencils, eh?"

No, Sunshine, *knives*! Kwai thought. But she smiled sweetly. "There's just one thing…"

"Speak."

"Can we bring a video recorder?"

"Of course. Anything, anything. But if you do, bring a long tape, luv. I adore the eye of the lens…"

"Thanks a lot. See you tomorrow, then."

"Can't wait, dear, can't wait." And Adam Bond skipped back to the stage in a much better frame of mind. "Come on, let's go from the girl's entrance," he said. "And concentrate, concentrate, *concentrate*!"

Which was Kwai's cue to slip away in the dusty dark, as if she didn't know Lucy from the girl in the moon.

Chapter Eight

It took a bit of lugging, the video, but Dean wouldn't let anyone else take the strain. Being macho man he wasn't going to let Sharon help – although she'd have made lighter work of it – and Mack would have bashed it against every lamp post down the street, he was in such a jumpy old mood.

"I ain't sure about this, mate," he kept on saying. "Could end us up in all sorts. Am I not 'appy about this…!"

But if he wasn't happy, Kwai had an extra dose of the cast iron *for* it. Adam Bond was a pig and a bully to Lucy; and he'd been ignorant and rude to her. If ever a person needed a public smacking on the bare backside – in a manner of speaking – it was Adam Bond.

Angelica was with her all the way; a man who brought the taste of salt into her mouth could take whatever was coming to him.

And that was what the video was all about.

Sharon, light on her feet and heavy with her hands, pushed open the door of the Samuel Pepys.

"Interview with Mr Bond," she announced to Mick the barman.

A couple of lunch time sleep-overs dipped their noses back into their beers.

"Oh, interviews, is it?" Mick asked. "Isn't it my life story you ought to be tellin'?"

"Even City East ain't ready for *your* life

story," Mack told him. "Get you run outta town double quick!"

"Ah, but think of it! Barmen carry the secrets of the mighty…"

"To their graves!" Dean came in – pulling Mack away from the stand-up double act. With Mack right now it was anything to put off the moment. "Can we go up?"

"Sure, they're all there, playing make believe."

"Then make believe you 'aven't seen us," Mack got out before Sharon pulled him by the shirt and Kwai pushed him in the back.

Sharon first, they went up and round the narrow stairs to the theatre.

Lucy was sitting in the tip-ups on her own. They'd fitted in a run of the play before the interview, and afterwards, they were going to have their notes and pick up on a few sticky scenes – all of which would be hers, of course.

Meanwhile, they were having a break.

"Ah, here comes the inquisition," Adam Bond announced.

"Do what?" asked Sharon.

"The press, luv. And I do hope you're going to be gentle with us."

"Like the kiss of a mozzy," Sharon told him. But he didn't hear her, because he was looking at what Dean was setting onto a table.

"You said a *video*," the Face puzzled.

"Yeah. This is. A video player."

"I thought you meant *camera*." Adam Bond turned for the laugh he knew he was going to get from the company. "I've had my hair done and put on some slap for this!"

Ho, ho, ho.

"We never said 'camera'."

"No, no, fine, fair enough. It's neat."

"It's one of those all-in-one jobs, play back only. My mum got it." Sophia had borrowed one of the play-back machines from Make-Up.

"As you like. So…" Adam Bond rubbed his hands, "how do you want to do this?"

"I've got the questions," Sharon waved a sheet of A4 at him, "and she's going to record the answers."

Kwai held up a small Sanyo recorder, like a game show assistant showing a prize to the studio audience.

"Well, we're all here, we're all ready to chip in," the Face told her.

"Only, it's mainly for you, son," Mack croaked out; then sat on the floor with his legs crossed, like a kid at Junior school. Well out of the way.

"What we want to do…" Sharon started, while Dean was being helped by Brenda the SM to plug in the equipment, "…is play you a couple of tapes and ask you about 'em."

"Like what?"

"Like, wait an' see. Eh?"

The Face gave a small and insincere laugh of disappointment. "But I thought you were going to cover the play – *Save Tomorrow For Me*." He looked at Amanda Flowers with shallow regret, hunched his shoulders.

"No, you're the target." Dean slotted in the first video tape. "It's you we're after."

Mack said something so low and desperate even he didn't hear what he'd said.

"So be it."

"Tape running," announced Kwai.

"Right, watch this," said Sharon, "then I'll ask you about it."

"Fair enough," said the Face – and gave a look of mock horror to the cast.

By now the room had settled. The company members were in the front row of the audience seats, with Adam Bond lounging in front in a stage armchair, looking so relaxed he had one hand touching the floor. And his eyes opened up like a happy flower as the first excerpt came up on the screen. This was going to be one lovely ego trip, his smile told the room.

Chapter Nine

The video picture was in colour, that over-bright studio colour of the early days. The setting was a police station, where two policemen were bringing in an arrested man – who, under the rags and tatters of a down-and-out's wardrobe, was none other than Adam Bond.

It was a short scene, set in Liverpool, and it was over quickly, the down-and-out giving off meths fumes and abuse, someone passing through before the main story suddenly jumped in. But it was a good piece of acting from the Face, playing a part he could really get his teeth into.

As Dean switched off the video recorder, the company clapped.

"Bravo!"

"More!"

"I remember that," said Amanda Flowers. "*Z Cars*. I didn't know it was you, in those days."

"*Very* good!" said Wig-on-a-Broomstick. "Centred. A lesson to us all."

"Oh, I go back…" said the Face, smug as you like at the clap.

"So, first question, how did you fit in with those others?" asked Sharon.

"I don't get you."

"They was on every week, wasn't they? Regular. Famous, my gran says."

"How did *they* treat *you*, being new?" Kwai

put in.

"Very well, they were very kind. A lot of laughs. Big stars don't treat character actors like rubbish, you know. We're all in the same job, however big or small our name is on the billing."

"'All…in…the…same…job…'" Sharon noted down.

"I've got it on the tape," Kwai called over.

"But that was ace important, don' you reckon?"

"Oh, I reckon," said Dean.

"Crucial," croaked Mack.

Angelica looked across at Lucy, who was at the end of the actors' row; Lucy with the face of a bone china plate, which right now was pinking, reddening, as she stared at the back wall, holding herself purposely out of focus.

"Right, can we have number two?" Sharon demanded.

"Number two!" Dean slotted in another cassette, while Adam Bond swivelled to it with the mellowist of looks, as if these kids were uncorking for him his favourite wine.

There was a countdown clock at the start of this tape, the one the studios put on and the public shouldn't see.

"Hello, what have you got here? This must be out of the archives."

The clock counted down.

"Eight, seven, six, five…" Someone always has to count down with it; and that someone had to be Mack.

The picture when it came up was in black and white; and the quality was poor. This was from the deepest archives.

Up came the title. *Poppy and Doppy's Playtime*, with a little jingle sung by two characters who were wagging their heads like crazy.

"Poppy and Doppy come to play,
A treat for you – every day.
I'm Poppy. I'm Doppy.
Here to say,
We're friends who never fade away."

"Strewth!" said Amanda Flowers. "I grew up with this."

"In your dreams, ducky," said Wig-on-a-Broomstick. "It's not *that* old. But who *were* these two sad cases. There's something famil-iar…"

Adam Bond knew. He was on his feet, as if a rat in the upholstery had bitten at the smell of fear. He was waving his hands, going for the video. "Sorry, if this is to be a *serious* inter-view…"

But Amanda Flowers suddenly screeched. "It's you!" she screamed. "Doppy – it's you! *Tell* me I'm wrong!"

Short of kicking in the set, there was

nothing the Face could do but back off at that, and sink into his armchair again – grinding his teeth with, "Early days, only a start…"

Now every eye was focused on the screen. Amanda Flowers was crawling towards it, on all fours like a dog in a Chummy ad. Wig-on-a-Broomstick had leaned so far forward, he fell.

All focused on Poppy and Doppy – but mainly on Doppy.

Poppy was a girl of about fourteen, dressed and made up like a rag doll. Doppy, now everyone could see, was who Amanda Flowers had said he was – a young Adam Bond, dressed up as a schoolboy in a round peaked cap and short trousers.

"This isn't in your programme notes," said Amanda Flowers. "You've left this off your list of successes."

"Oh, he wasn't Adam Bond then; he was

Colin Cloony," Dean told them; all matter of fact.

"Not unusual!" the Face snapped. "She's not Amanda Flowers, if it comes to that."

"There was already an Elizabeth Taylor," Amanda Flowers shot back. "What's your reason for changing?"

"Think you're gonna see," said Mack — voice up, and then down again.

On the screen, Poppy and Doppy were doing a routine with a cardboard car, teaching the tots how to cross the road safely...

"At the kerb, halt!" said Poppy. "What do I do now, Doppy?"

"Halt."

"Yes, I've done that." She gave him a quick look; sort of, where were you?

"Look left, look right..." Doppy had that caught-out face, like when a teacher asks a question in class and you've been thinking about the zit on your chin.

"No, we look right first, then left. We mustn't muddle our friends, Doppy."

"A slip! God, we've all done it!" Adam Bond moaned from low down in his armchair. "This *was* going out live…"

But the Adam Bond on the screen, the Colin Cloony, the Doppy schoolboy, was starting to sweat. He was looking off left, and looking off right, like someone caught in the middle of the road himself; while his young partner worked like an old pro to hold things together.

"So, what do we do, Doppy? At the kerb we– ?"

"Look right, look left…"

"We HALT!"

"Yes, first…"

"Well, first things first, eh? We– "

"Halt."

"Then?"

"Look left, look right."

"You've done it again, Doppy! I think Doppy means, look right, look left, doesn't he? Oh, you are being a silly old thing today."

Doppy did a dopey face, as if all this had been meant, written in the script — before he went suddenly out of view, like on the end of a hook. On the tape there was a silence, a cut-off silence, where the director must have taken out the studio sound to give a prompt. When it came back Doppy was saying, in an Adam Bond street voice, "Let's let Poppy tell us *properly*." Just his voice; the Face was out of vision.

Which was when Sharon shouted, "Cut!"

And Pepys Upstairs seemed to shout back, "Yes, please! CUT!"

Chapter Ten

The company was alive with the fleas of embarrassment; little bottom shuffles, their breathing kept thin, so as not to be the one to make a sound. Cast, SM, chaperone, lights and props, they were all there in the prickles. They looked like people praying for a catastrophe – *right now*.

Not Sharon, though. Perhaps she *was* the catastrophe.

"So, question two, what did that do for

your nerve, Mr Cloony? 'Cos you actors have to face out that sort of thing, don't you?"

The company squirmed. Why was she making him wriggle on the hook?

"Look –" Amanda Flowers started gamely, trying to come to his rescue.

But Adam Bond held up a hand to her. "Sure, we do have to face that. All of us."

"You mean, like, anyone can get hung up? Am I saying you right?"

"Yes."

Amanda Flowers groped for a fag and lit the wrong end.

"What we saw was, you lost it," Kwai said. "And you went from bad to terrible because your nerve was all gone."

"But you got over it," Dean put in. "You lost it in a big way there – but you bounced back on telly till you're who you are today. That's our direction, that's what we want to say in the paper, 'cos there's a lot of kids around who don't reckon they can hack it, once they've dumped in a test, or something..."

Adam Bond stood, a figure of less stature now, but taller somehow. He could have been playing a hero going to the stake.

"What I did happens all the time, but no one ever sees it, except on *Alright on the Night*. And people in the business understand. They're very supportive..."

"'Ow's that?" Mack put his spoke in. "'Ow do they make you feel all right?"

"Well, for me, a kind and understanding producer gave me a chance in something else, and he held my hand, and that led to something else again, and then something else..."

"That really is somethink else!"

"Everyone needs their hands held when they're going through a bad time," said Kwai.

"Better than being shouted at."

"True, very true. Well there," Adam Bond said, "you've made me bare my soul."

"Right on! It'll help some kids get in out of the rain, if the paper prints this." Sharon folded her A4 into razor sharp quarters.

"Hopefully," said the humble Adam Bond.

"Kids like Lucy!" Angelica exploded; who had the taste of salt still in her mouth; not sure in all of this whether they'd paid out Bully Bond or not.

"Kids like all of us, ducky," said Wig-on-a-Broomstick. "I'm scared gutless about opening night!"

At which everyone laughed. Lucy through her tears.

"Right! Enough! Notes tomorrow!" Adam Bond announced, heading for the door. "Ten thirty call. Break there for today." And he took the stairs two at a time down to the bar, where

Mick was quickly into offering glasses up to the whisky optic.

The company followed sharpish; while Lucy, Sharon, Angelica and Kwai went into a warm, tearful cuddle. Which Mack wormed into with a face that said never mind the jumps, he'd just found heaven. And which Dean found, too, nestled between Sharon and Kwai.

"You're real mates!" Lucy said. "I don't know what to say."

"I do, girl!" Mack told her. "At the kerb, halt. Look right, look left, an' when it's all clear– "

"Break a leg!" said Angelica; which got her a special hug from Lucy; before she suddenly broke it off.

Lucy was looking at Sharon; Sharon the fighter, Sharon the survivor, Sharon the no-rubbish taker. "We have assertion training at drama school, but nothing like that!" she told her.

"Just, some of us was born with it, sistuh!" said Sharon.

Lucy stared her straight in the eye. "And I'm going to adopt it right now! I'm going down there to get myself bought a Coke, on the company!"

And with kisses all round, she went for the stairs like someone walking out to collect an Oscar, head up.

"What about me? I could murder a Coke!" Mack said. "Closed shop, is it?"

Kwai patted his arm. "Let them get on with it now."

"Reckon we'll always be punters to them show boats," said Sharon. "Us this other side of the curtain."

Angelica shook her head. "Not with Lucy. She's different…"

Dean had nothing to say; he was heaving the video player to the door. "Here y'are, Mack," he said. "Your turn, mate."

"Ta a bundle, Mary-Ann." And Mack made as light of the burden as he could; helped by the fact that the walk back from the Samuel Pepys was a lot less jumpy than the walk there had been.

"Anyhow, cheers to your Auntie Pearl for remembering Colin Cloony!" said Kwai, trying to put a skip of celebration into her step.

"An' your ol' mum for diggin' it out of the studio," Mack told Dean.

"Taught him!" said Sharon. "But why do I feel flat?"

"'Cos he'll likely push his two tons with your editor mate." Mack rested the video for a spell. "Kill the story."

"Don' matter, we done it for Luce…"

"Tell you what," Mack had a flash, "let's

take an eel pie supper up my place, an' say ta to Auntie Pearl. Celebration!"

"Let's not," said Sharon, being honest. "Let's have a fizz in City Limits."

Which is what they did, raising their glasses with Renny and Sophia.

"To show biz," said Dean.

"To Lucy and the play," said Angelica.

And they all drank to that.

More

City
Limits

stories...

Bernard Ashley

STITCH-UP

Dean and Sharon are an item. She's sharp, funny and beautiful. Her half-brother is sharp too – sharp and dodgy. So when a robbery takes place right in front of him, Dean has some heavy-duty thinking to do. Does his loyalty to Sharon extend to her brother? Or is this a stitch-up?

CITY LIMITS 1

Bernard Ashley

MEAN STREET

A runaway gets Dean and Mack in a spin. She's a kid with attitude, a fighter, a survivor. Now Mack's comfortable bed gives him sleepless nights and Dean wants to forget he ever met her. Kwai's kindness only makes things worse. So can they help, will they help, a kid down on her luck on Mean Street?

CITY LIMITS 4